Dear Parent:
Your child's love of reading starts here!

I Can Read Books have introduced children to the joy of reading since 1957. Featuring award-winning authors and illustrators and a fabulous cast of beloved characters, I Can Read Books set the standard for beginning readers. From books your child reads with you to the first books they read alone, there are I Can Read Books for every stage of reading:

SHARED READING
Basic language, word repetition, and whimsical illustrations, ideal for sharing with your emergent reader

BEGINNING READING
Short sentences, familiar words, and simple concepts for children eager to read on their own

READING WITH HELP
Engaging stories, longer sentences, and language play for developing readers

READING ALONE
Complex plots, challenging vocabulary, and high-interest topics for the independent reader

ADVANCED READING
Short paragraphs, chapters, and exciting themes for the perfect bridge to chapter books

Every child learns in a different way and at their own speed. Some read through each level in order. Others go back and forth between levels and read favorite books again and again. You can help your young reader improve and become more confident by encouraging their own interests and abilities.

A lifetime of discovery begins with the magical words, **"I Can Read!"**

Hanukkah

selected by Lee Bennett Hopkins

An I Can Read Book™

Lights

HOLIDAY POETRY

pictures by Melanie Hall

HarperCollins*Publishers*

ACKNOWLEDGMENTS

Thanks are due to the following for use of works specially commissioned for this collection:

Curtis Brown, Ltd., for "First Candle" by Lee Bennett Hopkins; copyright © 2004 by Lee Bennett Hopkins. "One Little Miracle" by Jane Yolen; copyright © 2004 by Jane Yolen. Both reprinted by permission of Curtis Brown, Ltd.

Sandra Gilbert Brüg for "Five Little Dreidels" and "Goodnight." Used by permission of the author, who controls all rights.

Lillian M. Fisher for "Hanukkah." Used by permission of the author, who controls all rights.

Maria Fleming for "Dizzy" and "Winter Light." Used by permission of the author, who controls all rights.

Avis Harley for "Remember." Used by permission of the author, who controls all rights.

Peggy Robbins Janousky for "Shadows." Used by permission of the author, who controls all rights.

Michele Krueger for "Latke Time." Used by permission of the author, who controls all rights.

Ann Whitford Paul for "Spinning Hanukkah." Used by permission of the author, who controls all rights.

Phillip J. Tietbohl for "Taste of Hanukkah." Used by permission of the author, who controls all rights.

Hanukkah Lights: Holiday Poetry Text copyright © 2004 by Lee Bennett Hopkins Illustrations copyright © 2004 by Melanie Hall All rights reserved. No part of this book may be used or reproduced in any manner whatsoever without written permission except in the case of brief quotations embodied in critical articles and reviews. Printed in the United States of America. For information address HarperCollins Children's Books, a division of HarperCollins Publishers, 1350 Avenue of the Americas, New York, NY 10019. www.harperchildrens.com

Library of Congress Cataloging-in-Publication Data.
Hopkins, Lee Bennett.
    Hanukkah Lights : holiday poetry / selected by Lee Bennett Hopkins ; pictures by Melanie Hall.
       p.   cm.—1st ed.
    (An I Can Read Book)
    Summary: A collection of poems that celebrate the activities and experiences of Hanukkah.
    ISBN 0-06-008051-5 — ISBN 0-06-008052-3 (lib. bdg.) — ISBN 0-06-008053-1 (pbk.)
    [1. Hanukkah—Juvenile poetry. 2. Judaism—Juvenile poetry. 3. Children's poetry, American. 4. Hanukkah—Poetry.
5. American poetry—Collections.] I. Hall, Melanie W., ill. II. Title. III. Series.
PS595.H36 H35 2004   2003018901
811/.54 22   CIP
                                                                                                              AC

❖

To

Bobbye S. Goldstein—

brightest

of

lights

—L.B.H.

For the Goldfields,

with love

—M.W.H.

CONTENTS

DIZZY

BY MARIA FLEMING

I feel all giggly and wiggly
inside,
All twirly, whirly, squiggly
inside,
Like a dizzy top
dancing
and spinning
and humming,
Because Hanukkah
Hanukkah
Hanukkah's coming!

SPINNING HANUKKAH

BY ANN WHITFORD PAUL

I spin poems of Hanukkah,

my dreidel twirls them fast.

The menorah candles flicker

to help me make them last

for eight long nights.

I pile my poems on platters

carrying brisket, latkes, too,

and chocolate coins of money.

Now I serve my poems to you.

LATKE TIME

BY MICHELE KRUEGER

Grate the potatoes gently,

chop some onions, too.

It's time to make some latkes,

a heaping plate for you!

Heat the griddle slowly,

pour the oil in,

fry up forty latkes,

let the feast begin!

The oil's a reminder
of a story long ago
when lamps in a temple
continued to glow

longer than they should have.
Eight days of light!
We're celebrating Hanukkah
with latkes tonight!

TASTE OF HANUKKAH

BY PHILLIP J. TIETBOHL

Latkes for my friends.

Latkes for my aunts.

Latkes for my uncles.

Latke batter on my pants!

FIVE LITTLE DREIDELS

BY SANDRA GILBERT BRÜG

Five little dreidels:

One is silver bright

Two is worn and made of wood

Three is painted white

Four is round and chubby

Five is short and thin.

All with Hebrew letters—

nun, gimmel,

hay and *sh'in.*

WINTER LIGHT

BY MARIA FLEMING

When days are short,

And sun grows dim,

And night grows long,

And moon grows slim.

When it's dull,

When it's dark,

When a cold wind bites,

It's time for Hanukkah—

The Festival of Lights.

FIRST CANDLE

BY LEE BENNETT HOPKINS

The moment

first candle

is lit

light outshines

darkness.

ONE LITTLE MIRACLE

BY JANE YOLEN

One little light,

One cup of oil,

Restoring the temple

Took weeks of toil.

One little miracle,

One little light,

Lasting a lifetime

Night after night.

HANUKKAH

BY LILLIAN M. FISHER

Bring the shamash,

light a candle,

say the ancient prayer.

Spin the dreidel,

give the gelt,

gather loved ones near.

Tell it again and marvel—

"A miracle happened here!"

SHADOWS

BY PEGGY ROBBINS JANOUSKY

Shadows on our wall

Grow larger every night.

Another candle softly glows

Surrounding us in light.

We stand together hand in hand

A family of friends.

As one we voice a simple prayer:

May freedom never end.

REMEMBER

BY AVIS HARLEY

Glowing candles

write in gold

across the darkened

page of night

the ancient story,

richly told:

Menorah is remembered light.

GOODNIGHT

BY SANDRA GILBERT BRÜG

Soft, the candles glowing,

Music fills my head.

Frost is on the window

As I climb upstairs to bed.

Soft, the candles swaying,

Safe and warm the sight.

It's like the light is saying:

"Happy Hanukkah.

Goodnight."

Index of Authors and Titles